Scary Stories to Tell if You Dare 3

Sequel to

Scary Stories to Tell if You Dare
Scary Stories to Tell if You Dare 2

Collected from folklore and retold by Joe Oliveto
Illustration designs by Joe Oliveto
Copyright © 2020 by Joe Oliveto
All Rights Reserved

Table of Contents

THE CHASE

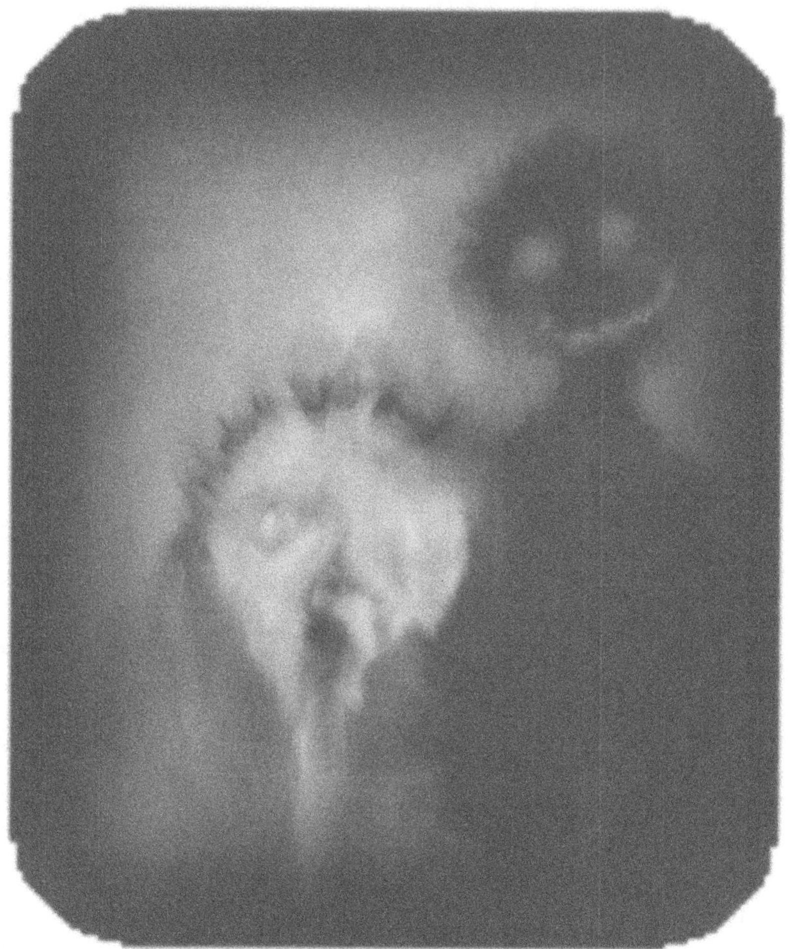

This happened when I was in high school. I was on the basketball team. Because we lived in a very rural part of the country, we would have to travel a very long way to play games against other schools sometimes. Usually, we would stay at a hotel overnight after a game if the trip was going to be very long, but there were some trips when the school didn't have enough money to pay for hotels.

This was one of those trips. After finishing up our game at another school many hours from our own, we all piled into the bus and headed back home. It was late at night and it would be a very long drive. Most of the others on the team fell asleep pretty fast. For some reason, I couldn't sleep very well, so I decided to just stay up and look out the window during the trip.

I lived near a Native American reservation back then. You couldn't see much of it in the dark night, but even so, I felt like I had to look out the window the whole time. It almost felt like something was looking back at me.

I should also point out that the bus driver was driving very fast at this point. He'd actually started driving very fast as soon as we got to the reservation. Before that point, he'd been taking it slow and safe.

What I saw next would have been strange no matter what. But it was even stranger when I remember how fast we were driving.

Out in the field next to the road I saw a figure running towards the bus. We were going more than seventy miles-per-hour at this point, but this figure seemed like it was gaining on us quickly. Once it got close enough I could see that its body was the shape of a person's, but it was very tall, its face was black, and its eyes were glowing.

The figure was now running alongside the road. It had no trouble keeping up with our bus, even though we were going so fast. It just stared at me with those terrible glowing eyes. I wanted to look away, or at least tell someone else about what I was seeing, but I couldn't seem to.

Then the thing started smiling at me. This wasn't any normal smile. It was an ear-to-ear smile, and beneath its lips, I could see the thing's horrible yellow teeth.

I don't know how long this lasted. It could have been just a few seconds, but it felt like it lasted hours. Finally, the thing fell to all fours. It looked like its bones were cracking inside of it, as if it was turning into some kind of animal. Hair started growing all over its body. After just a few seconds, whatever it was had turned into a coyote. I know what coyotes look like, having grown up near them, and that's exactly what I saw. It ran off into the night, and that's the last I saw of it.

THE WOMAN IN THE WINDOW

Charles Perry was a soldier in the Civil War. But he wasn't always fighting in battles. Sometimes his job was to go to nearby farms and houses to ask for supplies. Because of the war, people knew the army needed milk, eggs, water, and other things like that from time to time.

Charles was looking for houses to get supplies from one day when he found an old farm in a part of the county he had never been to before. Smoke was coming out of a chimney, so he knocked on the door and asked to come in.

No one answered. He knocked harder and told them he was a soldier who needed supplies for the army. Still, no answer.

At first he decided to look for another house. "Maybe whoever lives here left and forgot to put the fire out," he said to himself.

Charles started walking away when he noticed something in the upstairs window. A beautiful woman was looking down at him. She had flowing brown hair and wore a pink silk dress.

This made Charles change his mind. He forced his way into the farm and called out for the woman. "Why didn't you answer me?" he asked. "Don't you know I'm a soldier? We need supplies."

He didn't get a reply. But the fire was still burning and there was food at the table, so he was sure someone was in the house.

Charles headed up the stairs and called out for the woman, but still got no answer. He searched every corner of every room and couldn't find anyone.

"Maybe I'm just imagining things," he told himself. He was about to leave when he saw the woman out of the corner of his eye in one of the rooms. It looked like she snuck into a closet door he had missed when searching for her. But when he made his way over to that spot, there was no door at all. The wall was completely solid.

Charles decided to find the closest neighbor to ask about the woman he had seen. Pretty soon he reached another farmhouse about a mile away. An old woman came out to greet him.

"Who lives in the farmhouse a mile to the south?" he asked. "I saw a woman in there but now I can't find her."

The old woman seemed confused. "No one lives in that house anymore," she said. "A drunken soldier stopped by there a couple of years ago and killed the woman who lived in that farm when she wouldn't give him any money. It was very sad. She was a beautiful girl. She had pretty brown hair and always wore her best pink silk dress."

Charles couldn't believe it. He went back to the old farmhouse to see for himself. "That old woman must be crazy," he said.

But when he got there the smoke wasn't coming from the chimney anymore. Inside, there was no fire burning, and no food at the table. The place was dark and filled with cobwebs. The only sign that someone had ever been there was his footprints on the dusty floor.

THE CRYING BABY

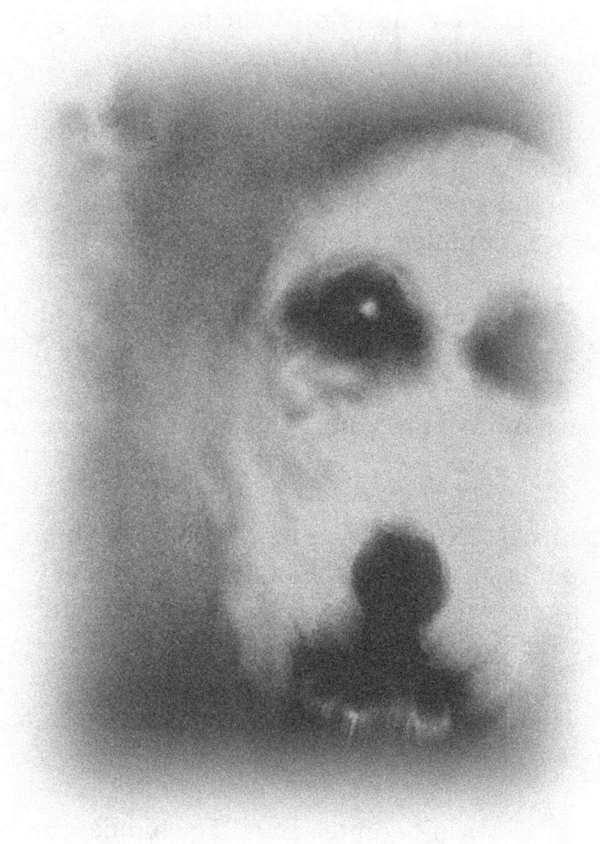

Lynne and Bobby's parents had gone out for the night, so Sam was babysitting them. Everything was normal for most of the night. They played games, watched TV, and told jokes.

By the time it was dark out they were all sitting around the TV downstairs watching a show. But soon they started to hear a noise that didn't sound like it was coming from the TV at all.

"Do you hear that?" Sam asked the children.

Bobby and Lynne both said they did. "It sounds like a baby crying outside," Lynne said.

Sam agreed that it did. The crying seemed to be coming from right outside the front door.

"You two stay here," Sam said. "I'm going to see what's wrong."

"Should we call the police?" Bobby asked.

"Wait for me to get back," Sam said. "I'll call them."

Sam headed upstairs and walked out the front door. A few seconds later, the crying stopped. But Sam didn't come back in right away.

"She's probably trying to calm the baby down first," Lynne said. "She'll be back."

But she didn't come back. Many minutes passed. Lynne and Bobby started to get very scared. They both looked out the window, but didn't see anyone. They thought about going outside to look for Sam, but they had been told to stay put. The children tried to call for her, but no one answered.

Bobby finally decided to call the police. When he told them what had happened, the officer on the other line told them to stay put. He was sending someone over right away. The officer made them promise not to go outside in the meantime.

The police got to their home very quickly. Bobby and Lynne asked where Sam was, but the officers wouldn't say anything until their parents got home. One officer sat with them around the TV while another waited outside by the door.

Bobby and Lynne's parents got home about an hour later. When they saw a police car in the driveway and an officer waiting at the door, they rushed inside and asked what was wrong.

The officers told them what happened. They told Bobby, Lynne, and both their parents to call the police if they ever hear a baby crying outside again. There was a killer loose in the state who was tricking people into coming outside by playing a recording of a baby crying outside people's homes. When someone came out to find out what was wrong, he would force them into his car and drive off with them. Only one person managed to escape so far. That's how the police knew about his trick.

The killer usually played his trick on babysitters.

A SHIP IN THE ICE

The *Octavius* was one of the grandest ships in the fleet. It was so grand, in fact, that even the captain's young wife and boy would come with him on some of his voyages, even when they were going to be away for very long.

This was the case on the ship's last known voyage. It was 1761, and the *Octavius* had sailed from London to transport a shipment of cargo to China. At first, the trip went as planned. The *Octavius* made it to China safely and the crew unloaded the cargo. Then the ship began the journey back to London.

Something must have happened on the return voyage, though. The *Octavius* never made it back home. For months, captains of other ships were told to keep an eye out for it, but no one could find any sign of the missing ship.

That changed in 1775. It had been nearly fifteen years since the *Octavius* had sailed from London to start its final voyage. The whaling ship *Herald* was sailing in the Greenland area, where both the water and the air were almost always as cold as death.

One day, the captain of the *Herald* spotted another ship not too far away. He ordered his men to sail towards it. The closer they got, the eerier the scene looked. The sails were tattered and there wasn't a sign of life to be seen. The crew tried hailing the ship, but they got no response.

The *Herald*'s captain decided they needed to go aboard the mysterious ship to see if anyone was alive. He and a few members of his crew walked a boarding plank to the deck of the ship, but they still found no one. Then they broke open the hatch to head below the deck.

What they found there chilled them to their bones. It was the bodies of twenty-eight crew members. Each and every one of them was frozen stiff.

As frightened as the *Herald*'s crew and captain were, they continued on, making their way into the captain's quarters. They found him there, frozen like all the others. He still had his pen in his hand, as if he'd died writing an entry into a journal or logbook. On the other side of the room, they found the frozen bodies of a woman and small boy.

The *Herald*'s men had seen enough. They grabbed the logbook from the captain's desk and ran back to their ship. When they calmed down, they began reading from the logbook. Although some of the pages had fallen out when they were running away, there was enough for them to learn what had happened to the mysterious ship they had just been aboard.

For reasons that weren't entirely clear, the captain of the ship had tried to take a different route home than he normally would have. Maybe there had been bad weather, or maybe he thought this route would get them home faster.

But none of that mattered anyway. The ship ended up getting caught in the ice of the northern waters. Because it somehow found its way to the waters off the coast of Greenland, it must have broken through the ice at some point. Sadly, before that happened, each and every soul on the ship had slowly frozen to death.

That was the last anyone saw of the *Octavius*. The crew of the *Herald* sailed back home and told the other sailors where they could find the ship that had gone missing so long ago. But, it seems the *Octavius* sank or kept drifting away, because no one was ever able to find it, and no one has ever seen it again.

Or, at least, that's what some say. There are others who claim the *Octavius* became one of the ocean's famous ghost ships. Some say if you're in the right spot, you can even catch a glimpse of *Octavius*, as the souls of its lost crew and captain spend the rest of time trying to find their way home.

A COLD FEELING

Jones was a student at the college a few hours away from where he grew up. That weekend he drove home to visit his grandmother. She'd raised him since he was a child, and she was feeling very sick, so he wanted to check in on her.

When Jones reached his grandmother's house he saw she was much sicker than she'd told him. "I have to take you to the hospital," Jones said. "You need to see a doctor."

"I don't need to go to a hospital," his grandmother said. "I'll be fine." She was an old-fashioned woman who thought she could take care of herself. Most of the time, Jones would let her make these types of choices on her own. But this time was different. He knew she'd get much worse if he didn't get her some help from a doctor.

Finally, Jones convinced his grandmother to let him drive her to the nearby hospital. He stayed with her for a few days, but he had a big test was coming up, so by Wednesday he had to drive back to the college.

His grandmother had been pretty calm during her time at the hospital, but when Jones said he was going to drive back to the college, that changed. She was very upset and asked him not to leave.

"I have to go back to school for this test," Jones said. "I'll be back here very soon."

The night Jones drove back to college was already a little cold, but as he drove back, he noticed that his car kept getting colder and colder. Much colder than he thought it should be. He turned up the heat, but it didn't do any good.

Then he saw something in the rearview mirror. When the car was at its coldest, he swore he saw his grandmother wrapped up in a blanket in the backseat. He parked the car and turned around to check, but there was no one there.

"It must have been my imagination," Jones thought. He started the car again and began driving back to the college. His friends were waiting for him in the parking lot as soon as he got there.

"There was a phone call for you," one of his friends said. "I think you should go and find out what it was about. We'll unpack your car."

Jones did as he was told. In the meantime, his friends took his bags up to his room. They noticed the inside of the car was very, very cold. Far too cold for that night.

When Jones got back to the room he told his friends what the phone call had been all about. It turned out his grandmother had died in the hospital while he was driving to the college. The doctors said she died at about seven o'clock that night. That was the same time he'd seen her in the rearview mirror.

CHOP

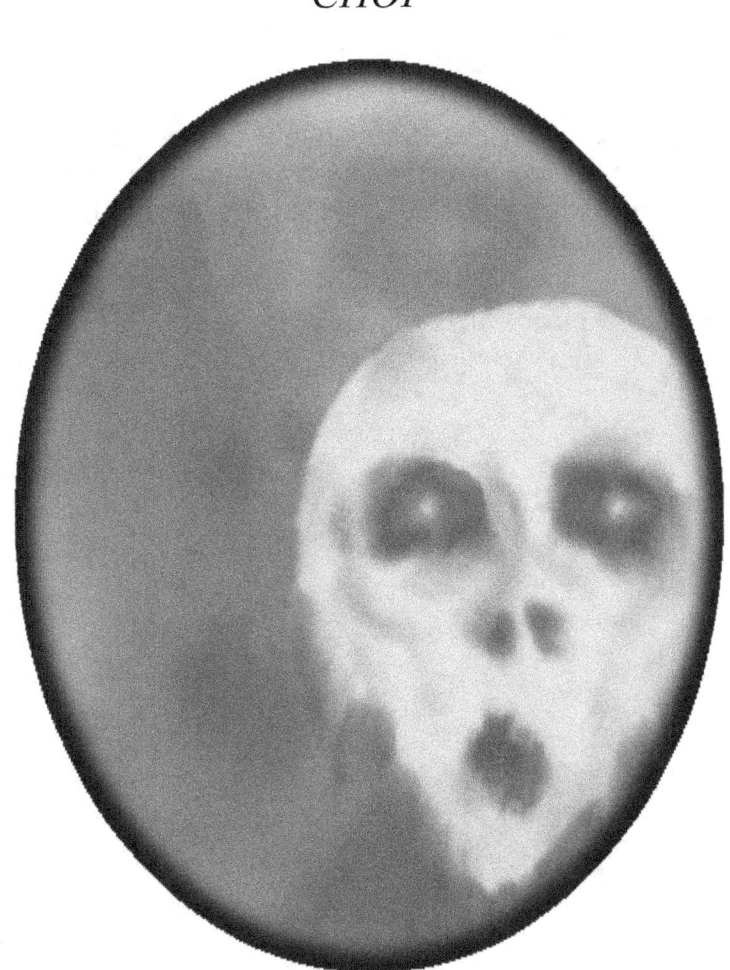

Sometimes brothers are like each other in many ways. But that wasn't the case with the Harrison brothers. One of them was a nice young man who was kind to everyone. The other was a mean brute.

When Mr. Harrison died he left the boys his farm. The nicer Harrison brother wanted to sell his half. This made his brother so angry he killed him with an axe. The farm had been in the family for years and years. He couldn't believe his brother would want to sell any of it.

He decided to hide his body under the floor in one of the farm's rooms. Later that year, he also married the girl his brother had been planning on marrying.

That's when strange things began happening at the farm. Any time the mean Harrison brother was near his wife, they would both hear a chopping sound. It would only go away when he was no longer very close to her.

This scared the young woman terribly. She had only lived in the farm one week when she told her husband she couldn't stand being so frightened anymore and needed to leave. She asked him to come with her, but he wouldn't leave his farm.

He tried to kill her instead. But she was luckier than the murdered Harrison brother. She managed to run away and get to a neighbor's farm.

When she told the neighbors about what happened, they went back to the Harrison farm to stop her husband from escaping before the police could arrive. However, when they got there, they found the evil Harrison brother was already dead. He'd hanged himself. Before doing so, it looked like he had pried up the floorboards.

In the floor was the body of the nicer Harrison boy. Next to him was an axe.

THE PRANK

During the first few weeks of college the frat would play pranks on the new students who wanted to become members. This had been going on for years. They needed to put their new members to the test to make sure they were serious about wanting to join.

Of course, that wasn't the only reason for the pranks. The older members of the frats also had a lot of fun laughing at the way their pranks and tricks would scare the younger students.

That's why they were so unhappy with one student who wanted to become a member of their frat. His name was Jeremy, and nothing they did seemed to bother him very much. Tricks that would terrify others didn't seem to scare Jeremy at all.

So, one day, a few members of the frat decided they would play their scariest prank yet on Jeremy. They showed up at his dorm saying they wanted to take him for a ride out to the country. They said there was something he needed to do out there if he really wanted to join the frat.

Jeremy agreed, but he already seemed a little more frightened than he usually would be, since he didn't say very much for the entire ride.

After about half an hour of driving, they reached an old abandoned house. It was very dark out now.

"We're going down to the basement," the driver of the car said. "We have to show you something down there, Jeremy."

They all went down to the basement, two of them holding Jeremy by the arms to make sure he wouldn't run away. The driver carried a bag with him. Jeremy wasn't sure what could possibly be in it.

When they got down to the basement, they needed flashlights to see. It looked like all that was down there was a small bed.

"Get on the bed, Jeremy," the driver said. "You have to do this if you want to be part of our frat."

At first, Jeremy didn't move, but he figured this was just a prank, and he'd be fine. But when he got on the bed, the boys suddenly held him down. They tied his arms and legs to the bed so tight he could barely move. Then they put a gag in his mouth and a blindfold over his eyes.

"Don't worry, Jeremy," the driver said. "All we're going to do is cut your arm a little so we can get a few drops of blood. We need to know you have what it takes to be a member of our frat."

Jeremy tried to struggle, but he was tied up so tight that he couldn't do anything. In the meantime, the driver took out a knife. He never actually planned on cutting Jeremy. Instead of using the sharp side of the blade, he ran the dull, flat side of the blade along Jeremy's arm. One of the other boys poured a little bit of cold water over the spot where the driver had run the knife along Jeremy's arm to make him think he'd actually been cut. They knew Jeremy was so scared he wouldn't realize the water wasn't actually his blood. They all had to try very hard not to laugh while they played their trick.

They had also set up a pan beneath Jeremy's arm so he would hear the water dripping down. They tied the water bottle to a rope hanging from the ceiling and tilted it just perfectly so it would continue to slowly drip water onto the pan. That way, Jeremy would hear the dripping and think he was still bleeding.

"We're going out for a little bit," the driver said. "We should be back in a few hours. Don't bleed too much, Jeremy! We hope none of the rats down here get to you while we're out."

The older members of the frat went driving around for a while, joking about how badly they'd finally scared Jeremy. They couldn't wait to see the look on his face when they got back.

But when they finally did get back to the basement, that all changed. Jeremy was so still that it almost looked like he'd fallen asleep. When they took off the blindfold and mouth gag they could see his face was frozen in a look of complete fear. They tried to get Jeremy to snap out of it, but he wouldn't respond.

The frat members got kicked out of the school after that. The doctor had told them Jeremy died of fright.

THE FIGURE IN THE ROOM

The old woman had not been sleeping well for weeks. She lived with her daughter, and her daughter had been very sick. The woman had spent so much time caring for her that she never had a chance to get much rest. Because of this, when she did finally go to bed at night, it usually wouldn't take her very long to fall asleep.

One night, she was just about to fall asleep, when she heard a noise that worried her. The woman listened closely. It sounded like someone was walking up the stairs from the lower level of the house. Then it sounded like it was walking down the hallway towards her room.

Her room was so dark that she could barely see anything. But a moment after the footsteps reached her door, she thought she saw a figure step inside. It only stayed a short moment before walking to her daughter's room. It sounded like the figure opened a drawer quickly before closing it. After that, it left the daughter's room and went back downstairs and out the front door. Again, it was very dark, but it had almost looked like the figure was now carrying a piece of her daughter's clothing with it.

Normally the woman would have rushed to her daughter to see if she was okay. This time, though, she'd been so close to sleep that she believed it must have been a dream. She'd been so worried about her daughter's illness that it was no surprise she was having nightmares.

However, the same thing happened the next night. Now the woman wondered if it truly had been a dream, but she still decided it probably was. She chose not to mention anything to the rest of the family or her daughter. Everyone else had also been very worried, and she didn't want to give them reason to worry even more.

Then it happened again. On this night, the woman knew she wasn't awake, so it couldn't have been a dream, but she still thought maybe she was just imagining what she had seen. When she heard the figure walk out the front door she looked out her window to see if she could get a better look at it in the moonlight.

It was definitely real. The figure slowly walked to the churchyard across the street. That's when she lost sight of it.

That was the last night the figure appeared. Instead, the woman's daughter died the next night. The family buried her in the churchyard.

FOG

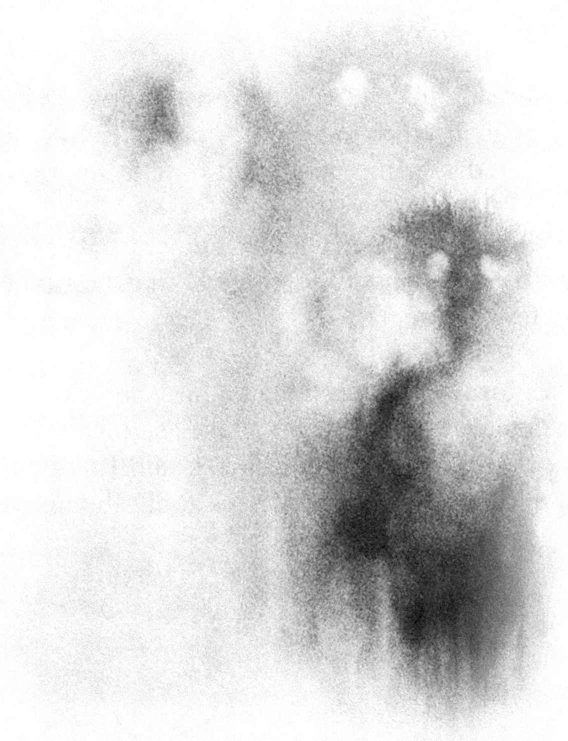

No one knew why Crab Orchard Cove was always so foggy. Some of the older people in town thought it was because the place was haunted. Others said there had to be a natural reason for the fog.

Mr. Baker was one of those people. He owned a farm near Crab Orchard Cove. No one was going to tell him his land was haunted. His children, Tommy and Suzy, believed the stories about the hauntings, but Mr. Baker told them there was nothing to be afraid of.

One morning, Mr. Baker sent the two children out to the fields to collect some wood for the fire. They were afraid of doing so since it was so foggy, but he told them they could take their big dog Blackie with them. That made them feel a little safer.

It was a quiet morning except for the sound of birds chirping and Blackie barking. Sometimes when he was roaming around the fields it seemed like he was barking at things they couldn't see.

Tommy and Suzy had started to feel less worried. It was fun to be out playing in the fields with Blackie. But suddenly, he stopped and looked deep into the fog.

"What do you see, boy?" Tommy asked.

Blackie stood still for a moment, then ran fast into the fog, barking as he went. In just a few seconds Tommy and Suzy couldn't hear him barking at all anymore.

They were afraid of the fog, but they were more afraid of losing Blackie. They ran into the fog calling after him. But he was nowhere to be found.

Tommy and Suzy were about ready to cry over their lost dog when he slowly walked out of the deep fog into a spot a few feet away from them. They called to him, asking him to come back, but the fog around Blackie started swirling up around him. Soon, they couldn't see him again.

That would be the last time they would see Blackie. They ran over to the spot where he stopped, but once more, there was no Blackie. This time, though, they could hear him. The dog whined like it was very scared for a few moments.

Blackie stopped making any noise soon after that. Tommy and Suzy spent a long time looking for him in the fog, but they couldn't find him. Mr. Baker said he must have run away, but he knew that wasn't like Blackie. He'd always been such a faithful dog. From then on, Mr. Baker thought that maybe there was some truth to the stories about the hauntings in the fog.

GLOWING EYES

Something strange had been happening at the mine for weeks. Miners working near the slope where the mine began would spot an odd-looking animal from time to time. It was grey, furry, and about five feet tall and eight feet long. It stood on all fours. What made it truly frightening were its eyes. They were bigger than the eyes of any other animal from those parts, and they glowed as bright as a car's headlights.

Whenever the animal showed up it would do the exact same thing. It would simply walk up the start of the slope, look down into the mine for a few seconds, then head back to the mountain. But every single time the animal came to the mine, about fifteen minutes or so would pass, then there would be a slate fall and a few miners would die.

Some of the men would try to kill the animal as it walked back to the mountain. But no matter how many times they shot it, they never could seem to do any harm. The animal would simply look back at them for a moment, then keep walking.

Everyone figured the animal must have had something to do with all the deaths at the mine. They believed that if they could kill it the deaths would stop.

So, the mine owner hired two of the town's best hunters, Bill and Jack, to go kill the animal. They headed up to a shack in the woods with powerful rifles and some food. They waited for a long time, but finally, they saw animal head down to the mine. They shot at it, but even with their very strong rifles, they still couldn't hurt it.

When the animal got to the slope of the mine it looked down into it for a lot longer than it normally would. Then it left.

Bill and Jack started shooting at it again when it passed by their shack and back into the mountain. No matter what, none of their bullets seemed to do any harm.

That didn't matter, though. Just a few moments later, Bill and Jack heard a loud roar coming from the mine. They ran to see what it was.

The mine had exploded. Twenty-two men had lost their lives. But that was the last time anyone saw the animal.

THE BANANA

A mother came home from the market with some bananas one day. She gave one to her son with his lunch and told him to eat it while she did chores in the other room.

A few minutes later her son came to tell her the banana was moving on its own.

"Don't be silly," she said. The mother thought her son was just being picky. "Eat your lunch."

The boy went back to the dining room to do as he was told. His mother went back to her chores, but a moment later she heard her son screaming. Then there was a loud thud.

She rushed to the dining room and found him lying unconscious on the floor. There were two small dots of blood on his hand.

The mother quickly drove her son to the doctor. She gave the boy some medicine and told his mother he would wake up soon. The doctor said the boy was lucky to be alive. He'd been bitten by a very dangerous snake. If the mother got to the doctor any later, the boy might have died.

Both of them wondered how that type of snake could have gotten into the mother's home. Those types of snakes usually didn't live in this area. Where did it come from?

They got their answer when the boy woke up. He told them when he unpeeled the banana that was moving on its own, a snake slithered out and bit him.

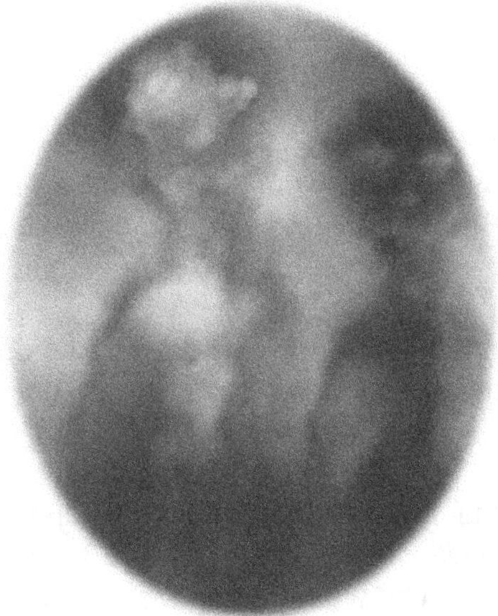

When they went back to the house, they found the hatched snake egg still in the banana peel.

THE SOLDIER'S CORPSE

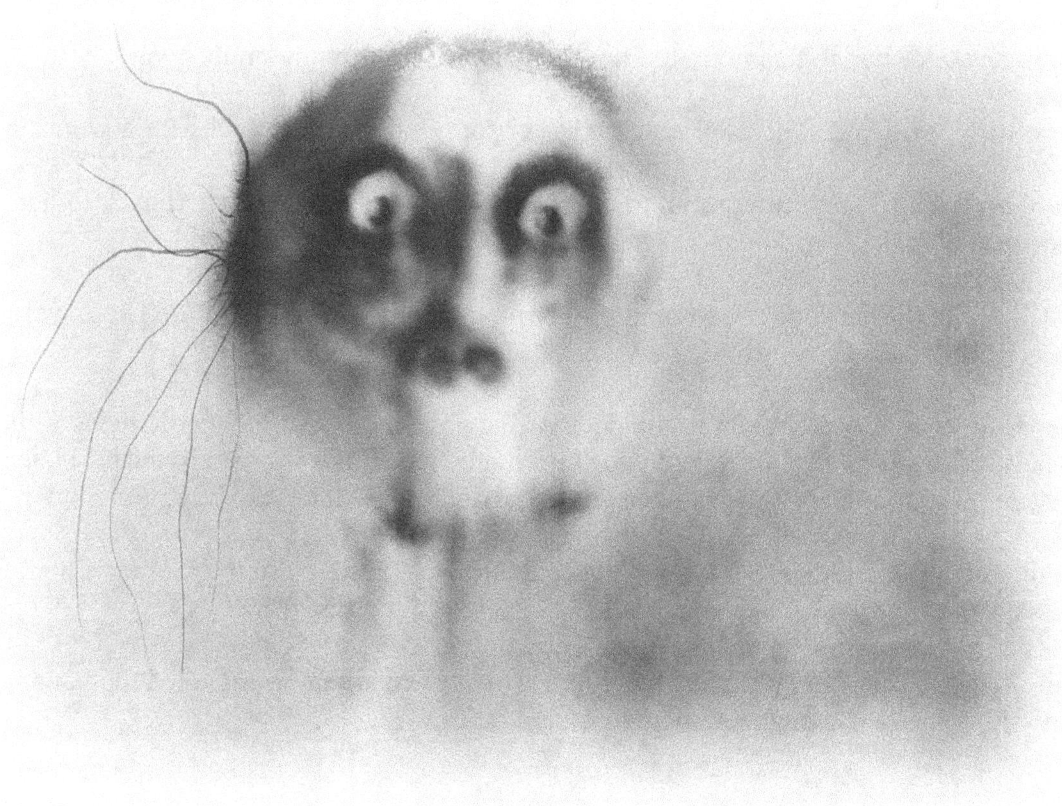

This happened during the Civil War. Some wounded soldiers had camped out near a small town to wait for the doctor to arrive. But it took him a long time to reach them, and by the time he did, one of the soldiers had died. The doctor took him to the undertaker.

The undertaker had a very busy night ahead of him. Because he didn't have time to preserve the dead soldier's body right away, he put it in a tub with ice water. That would keep it preserved until he had time to do his work.

The body stayed in the tub like that until morning. That's when the undertaker started the work of preserving it for a burial. He began by sewing the corpse's mouth shut. Then he placed a needle and tube into each arm. One tube would pump the fluid that preserves corpses into the body. The other tube would drain the corpse's blood.

That's as far into his work as the undertaker got. Suddenly, the corpse sat right up. When he noticed the tubes in his arms he pulled them out. It also looked like he was trying to talk, but he couldn't with his mouth sewn shut.

But all this only lasted a moment. The preserving fluid had already been pumped into the soldier's corpse. It was poisonous, and soon, the soldier settled back down. The look on his face seemed to be that of a man who knew he was dying, and had accepted it.

Many odd things started happening at the undertaker's office soon after. The undertaker would leave a room, and when he came back, he would see that furniture had been moved, even though there was no one in the shop to move it. Sometimes even bodies had moved.

That wasn't all. The undertaker had to start hiding the fluid and needles he used to preserve corpses. But no matter where he hid it, the fluid would go missing. All he would find in its place were bent needles.

This was all a little funny to many of townspeople. They thought some practical joker must have been behind what was going on at the undertaker's officer.

But it wasn't funny to the undertaker. He knew it had something to do with the soldier whose corpse had suddenly come to life, and in less than a year, he'd gone insane.

A BABY IN THE WOODS

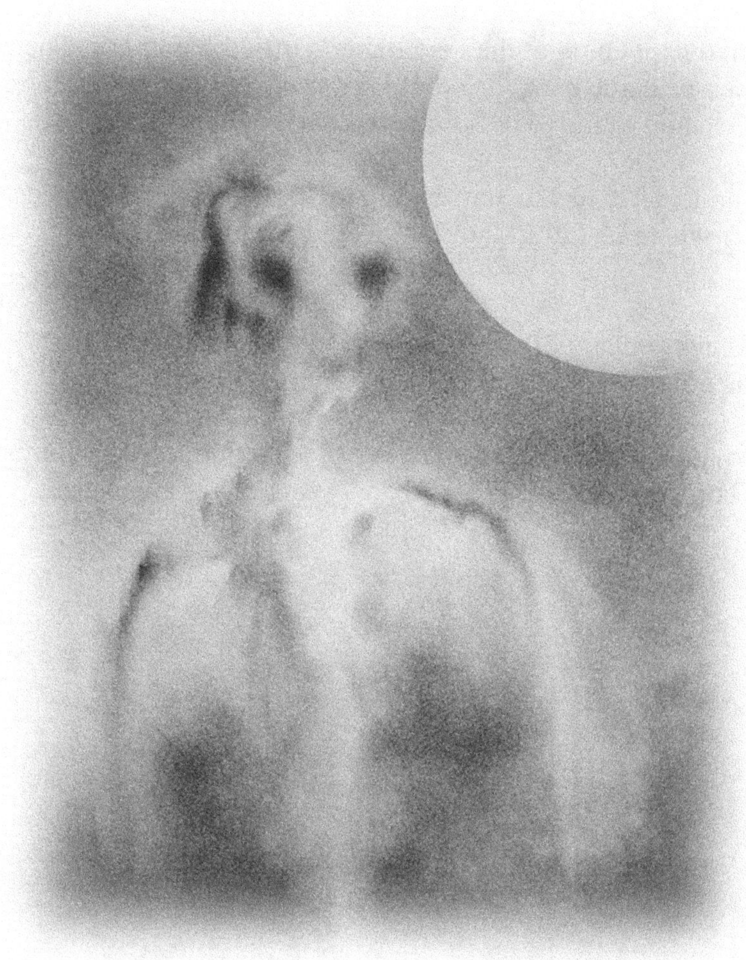

Odette lived in the Louisiana backwoods with her husband Alcide. Both of them wanted a child more than anything else in the world. Sadly, they could never seem to have one.

That didn't stop Odette from praying for a child. She'd go to church to pray whenever she could.

One day she was in a hurry so she took a shortcut to get to church. It was a path through the woods. Odette had never taken it before because her grandmother had warned her years ago not to.

"Don't ever take that shortcut," she would say. "The Devil lives in those woods."

Odette listened to her grandmother as a child. But now she was older. She didn't really believe those stories anymore.

On her way down the path, Odette noticed some beautiful flowers. "Maybe if I gather some of these flowers and bring them to church as an offering, God will give me a child," she said to herself.

Odette got so busy walking along and gathering flowers that she almost didn't notice the path was actually taking her deeper into the woods. She thought that was strange, because it was supposed to be a shortcut.

As she thought this, Odette began to hear the sound of a baby crying. She looked around until she spotted a bundle under a nearby tree.

Odette ran over and found a baby wrapped up in the bundle. "You poor thing," she said. "Someone must have abandoned you out here."

As soon as Odette picked the baby up, it stopped crying and started laughing.

This was the answer to her prayers. If someone left the baby out here, she would bring it back to Alcide and they would raise it as their own.

She began hurrying back home. The baby was still laughing. Then she stopped when she realized she had forgotten to thank God for giving her this child.

Odette placed the baby down in its bundle and started thanking God. As soon as she began praying, the child began crying. The more she prayed, the louder the crying was.

"Maybe it's hungry," she said. "I'll get the baby home to feed it."

Odette picked the bundle back up and unwrapped it. But now there wasn't a baby inside anymore. Instead, it was some sort of insect-like thing, like a giant beetle with shiny skin.

It began growing into her arms instantly. Odette was so terrified she dropped the bundle on the ground. At first, she couldn't move. She could only stand there and watch the thing grow before her eyes.

Finally, she started praying again. This made the thing howl in anger and terror. By now it looked like a large man with the skin of an insect. It ran off back into the woods, and Odette ran to church. She thanked God for letting her get away.

Odette and Alcide moved to another part of the state after that. Soon they had a child, and another, and another, until they had a big family. Odette prayed her thanks every night, and made sure never to wander into the woods again.

THE HANDPRINT

Mr. Harvey had a big house that everyone in town was jealous of. One man, Mr. Stanley, always tried to buy it from him.

"You're too old to take care of a place like this," he would say to Harvey. "I'm much younger and stronger. Let me buy it from you so you can move somewhere warmer."

Harvey told Stanley he would sell the house to him one day, when he was ready to move. But after years and years, he still hadn't sold it.

Until one day he was gone. No one knew what happened.

Stanley moved into the house shortly after. He told people Harvey had finally sold it to him and moved to a warmer part of the country.

People knew Harvey was a private person. They also knew he had said he planned on selling the house to Stanley when he was ready. So, no one asked too many questions when Stanley moved in.

The house was very big for one person. Stanley decided he could make some extra money by renting out one of the rooms. A young couple named McCarthy took the room pretty quickly.

It was a nice place to live. Stanley didn't charge them very much for the room. Every day, he fed them potatoes from a large sack he kept in the cellar.

There were only two things the McCarthys didn't like about living there. First, Stanley was just as private as Harvey. He made them promise never to go in the cellar without him.

"What if we're hungry for potatoes and you're not home to get them?" they would ask. But Stanley told them they would just have to wait.

The other problem was the strange red handprint on the hallway wall. It never went away. Stanley would try to paint over it, but the handprint would always come back.

One day Stanley was out for a long time. The McCarthys were getting very hungry. They decided to go down to the cellar for potatoes, even though Stanley told them not to. He wouldn't find out if they went down fast and only took a few.

The cellar smelled horrible. The McCarthys wanted to get their potatoes and get out of there as quickly as possible. They were taking potatoes out of the sack and were almost ready to head back upstairs when they noticed a strange shape poking out from beneath the big potato sack.

After looking at it more closely, they realized it was a boot. They immediately rushed out of the house and found a neighbor to let them in. The McCarthys called the police and told them what they saw.

When the police went down into Stanley's cellar, they lifted the potato sack up and found the body of Harvey beneath it. Stanley had killed him, hiding the body under the sack because he didn't want neighbors to spot him burying it. Strangely, the handprint on the wall was the same size as Harvey's hand.

It never went away. After Stanley went to prison, other people lived in the house, but no one could paint over the handprint. It stayed there until the house burned down many years later.

THE SAILOR'S VISIT

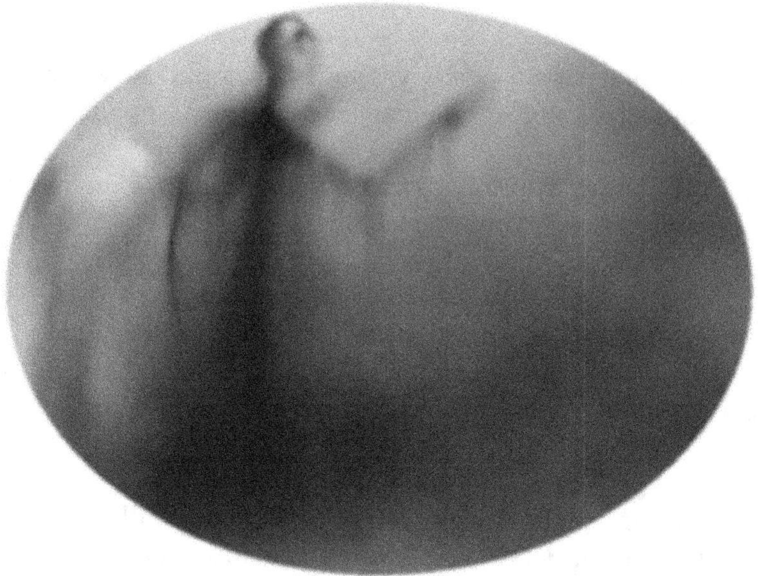

There was once a woman who lived alone near the coast. Even when she'd been married, she'd spent much of her time alone, because her husband was a sailor. When he got back home from his voyages, she would know it was him right away from the sound of his footsteps. He usually wouldn't say anything, because it would often be late at night when he reached their house, and he thought she was asleep. He didn't want to wake her.

Even though most of the time she was awake and waiting in bed for him to return, she would pretend to be asleep. She knew he was very tired after his voyages. Instead of keeping him awake with questions, she would wait until the morning to talk to him.

One late night when she was expecting him to return home it was very stormy. She knew when he got home he'd probably track mud onto the floor and she'd have to clean it up, but she didn't mind. She was just happy he would be back.

She was lying in bed when she heard him walk in the front door as expected. The familiar sound of his footsteps made its way from downstairs up to her bedroom. When they reached the bed, she heard him take his boots off, then felt him lie down next to her. The woman couldn't wait until the next morning when she'd be able to talk to him about his voyage. Right now, though, she would go to sleep.

But she woke up earlier than usual the next morning. A phone call had woken her.

"Who could be calling at this hour?" the woman asked herself.

When she picked up the phone, the police were on the other end. They told her they had bad news. Her husband's boat had sunk in the storm. He and the rest of the crew had died.

"That's impossible," the woman said. "My husband came home last night. He's in bed right next to me."

However, the woman had never actually bothered to look next to her to see if her husband was there. The phone call had woken her up so suddenly that she was still tired and never thought to check.

When she looked over, her husband was nowhere to be found. The woman hung up the phone and searched the house for him. She called out his name, but got no answer.

This went on for hours. Finally, the police showed up at her house and said they had her husband's corpse. It had washed ashore with the bodies of the other crew members. They needed her to go with them because someone who knew him had to say for sure that the body was his.

The woman went along with the police. She was more worried now, but she still couldn't believe her husband was dead.

Sadly, the body was his. Of course, this made the woman deeply sorrowful. But it also made her frightened, and a little confused. When she was searching the house earlier she hadn't found her husband, but she found a sign that he had certainly come home the night before: a series of muddy boot prints leading from the front door to her bed. They were the exact same size and shape as her husband's boots.

THE TUNNELS

All the kids knew about the tunnels beneath the city. Most cities have sewer tunnels, but these were different. Some people said they were built over a hundred years ago as hiding places in case a war ever broke out. Others heard they used to be part of a secret underground prison.

Most of the adults in the city knew they were actually old mine tunnels. Rich people used to build them for stone mines, and the tunnels became so big they wound up connecting with each other. They ran on for miles.

Over time, people stopped using them for mining. Now they were just a giant underground maze.

The adults knew the tunnels weren't safe because they were so easy to get lost in. But that wasn't the reason most of the kids thought the tunnels were dangerous. They'd all heard stories about the tunnels being haunted, or about insane killers who lived in them, or even about monsters that would eat a person alive.

One night some of the kids were telling each other these stories at a party. Most of them took the stories seriously. Except for one girl, Masha. She even said it would be fun to explore the tunnels.

"I'll go down there right now and prove there's nothing to be scared of. Maybe some of you will even be brave enough to join me. We'll just stay for an hour."

Two others agreed to go with Masha. They all headed out to one of the nearby entrances to the tunnels. It was already dark, and they knew the tunnels would be even darker, so they all brought flashlights.

When they walked down into the tunnels, the first thing they noticed was how confusing they were. Because different people had built them over the years, some sections were very small, and others were very wide. Sometimes a part of the tunnel would seem to go on for miles, and another would lead to a dead end right away.

The two who'd gone in with Masha quickly realized it would be very easy for them to lose their way if they kept going deeper into the tunnels to explore them. There wasn't that much to see anyway. There weren't any ghosts, killers, or monsters. Just miles and miles of brick walls.

Masha was still curious, though. "Come on," she said. "I want to get some good pictures to show everyone."

The others wouldn't go any further. They'd already seen enough.

"Okay, fine," Masha said. "We said we'd stay for an hour, so you two stay here. I'm going to walk around a little more."

Masha started walking deeper into the tunnels. After about a minute, the others couldn't see the glow from her flashlight any longer.

A half hour passed. Then another. Masha should have been back by now. They started calling out to her, but they never got an answer. This went on for almost another half an hour. That's when they decided to go back to the party and let everyone know what happened.

When they told their story, the other kids decided they had to tell their parents about Masha. The adults called the police, who spent the next few weeks looking for Masha in the tunnels.

She never showed up. No one ever saw Masha again. All the kids told stories about her. Some said a killer or a monster must have found Masha. Some even claimed if you went down into the tunnels you could still hear her crying for help some nights.

But most people knew the truth. It wouldn't have mattered if a killer or monster had really found Masha in the tunnels. They went on for miles. Masha probably just got lost. In the dark, she took too many wrong turns, and never found her way out. She's probably still in there, but by now, she would just be a skeleton.

NOTES AND SOURCES

THE CHASE
An account on Reddit serves as the inspiration for this retelling. The story describes a supposed encounter with a skinwalker (or skin-walker) from Navajo legend.

It's important to understand that those who are not Navajo themselves tend to have a limited understanding of the true nature of skinwalkers. I have no Navajo heritage, and don't wish to give readers the impression that I thoroughly understand Navajo legends and beliefs.

That said, in general, those outside the Navajo culture would typically understand the skinwalker as being a type of witch. Skinwalkers can change their shape, and some claim they are more likely to appear if you've been talking or thinking about them. In general, though, it's best to research the topic in greater detail if you find it interesting, as modern accounts of skinwalker encounters may not always be accurate reflections of Navajo beliefs.

This story also highlights how the Internet has contributed to the way in which we share folklore. Stories like those found in this book used to be shared around the campfire. Now, we can share our folklore online.

Source: u/Iron_Jesus. "Navajo Skinwalker encounter on a bus." *r/skinwalkers,* Advance Publications, 26 February 2014

THE WOMAN IN THE WINDOW
Alvin Schwartz's *Scary Stories to Tell in the Dark* included "The Guests." That was another story in which a home's haunted history intruded on the present day.

(Or, at least, the present day of the story.)

These types of creepy stories from folklore are common. They suggest that hauntings may be so strong they even change the way we experience the physical world.

Source: Musick, Ruth Ann. *Coffin Hollow and Other Ghost Tales*, The University Press of Kentucky, 1977

THE CRYING BABY
Many urban legends involve babysitters facing very real-world dangers. As Alvin Schwartz pointed out in his original *Scary Stories* books, these stories may be so common because babysitting is an almost symbolic experience.

A babysitter is typically a young person who is finally old enough to be the (short-term) guardian of someone younger. Facing the responsibilities of adulthood also involves facing the fears of adulthood. This may be why the dangers in babysitting urban legends usually aren't supernatural in nature. A young person being introduced to one of their first adult roles must struggle with the anxiety those roles naturally involve.

Source: Brunvard, Jan Harold. *Be Afraid, Be Very Afraid*, W.W. Norton & Company, 2004

A SHIP IN THE ICE

Like many stories about ghost ships, some believe there's truth to the story of the *Octavius*. That may not be the case, but it's possible such stories became widespread because sea voyages have always been dangerous. Many scary stories serve as exaggerated reflections of real fears.

Source: Harvey, Ian. "The mystery of the Octavius: An 18th-century ghost ship was discovered with the captain's body found frozen at his desk, still holding his pen." *The Vintage News*, The Vintage News, 30 October 2016

A COLD FEELING

If you spend enough time reading people's personal accounts of creepy experiences, you'll find many have had the experience of unexpectedly seeing a loved one at the moment of their passing. In many such stories, these ghostly apparitions appear in bedrooms and startle those seeing them from their sleep. This often makes the person having the experience suspect it was a dream. Only after they hear of their loved one's passing do they consider the possibility that it was their spirit saying goodbye.

However, while many of these stories are comforting, suggesting a person wishes to let their family and friends know they're passing on to the other side, this one touches on feelings of guilt. This makes it unique from other stories of this nature.

Source: Jones, James Gay. *Haunted Valley And More Folk Tales of Appalachia*, James Gay Jones, 1979

CHOP

Creepy stories about murder victims driving their killers to death are very common in American folklore. I found many stories like this when researching what to include in this collection, but the simplicity of this one made it the best choice.

Source: Musick, Ruth Ann. *The Telltale Lilac Bush and Other West Virginia Ghost Tales*, The University Press of Kentucky, 1965

THE PRANK

Fans of the original *Scary Stories to Tell in the Dark* books might find similarities between this story and "The Curse" or "The Dead Man's Hand" from *More Scary Stories to Tell in the Dark*. As with urban legends about babysitters, stories about fraternity initiations going terribly wrong touch on genuine fears young people may have about the dangers they'll face as they become adults.

Of course, these types of urban legends also serve as warnings. Fraternity initiations have genuinely resulted in deaths. Stories like "The Prank" remind us that "fun and games" can turn deadly.

Source: Brunvard, Jan Harold. *Be Afraid, Be Very Afraid*, W.W. Norton & Company, 2004

THE FIGURE IN THE ROOM

Like "A Cold Feeling," this is another story about a harbinger of death. It might reflect the fears and anxieties people have as they watch loved ones struggle with deadly illnesses. The visit of a specter in the night is a supernatural manifestation of the dread we may experience when we feel a loved one is near death, and there's nothing we can do about it.

Source: Musick, Ruth Ann. *The Telltale Lilac Bush and Other West Virginia Ghost Tales*, The University Press of Kentucky, 1965

FOG

Experts on the subject of horror and creepy tales from folklore often suggest that ghosts, monsters, and other such mythical beings can be symbols of our deep subconscious fears. This might be the reason everything from old ghost stories to modern horror films link fog with mysterious happenings. We know there's something terrifying lurking within it, but we don't (and maybe can't?) know exactly what it is.

Source: Jones, James Gay. *Haunted Valley And More Folk Tales of Appalachia*, James Gay Jones, 1979

GLOWING EYES

Again, scary supernatural stories are often reflections of actual fears rooted in real-world anxieties. The truth is, coal mining has always been a dangerous occupation, and it was extremely dangerous when we didn't have today's technology to keep workers relatively safer. This type of story might have become ingrained in West Virginia folklore because it translated a very real hazard into monstrous being.

Source: Musick, Ruth Ann. *The Telltale Lilac Bush and Other West Virginia Ghost Tales*, The University Press of Kentucky, 1965

THE BANANA

Anyone who enjoyed this story should revisit "Sam's New Pet" from Alvin Schwartz's *Scary Stories 3: More Tales to Chill Your Bones*. It's likely no coincidence that the fruit infested with a snake in this story also happens to be one many Americans associate with certain other parts of the world. As many urban legend and folklore experts suggest, these types of urban legends could reflect fears of immigrants.

Noted folklorist Jan Harold Brunvard included this story in his collection *Be Afraid, Be Very Afraid*. His work is essential reading for anyone with an interest in urban legends.

Source: Brunvard, Jan Harold. *Be Afraid, Be Very Afraid*, W.W. Norton & Company, 2004

THE SOLDIER'S CORPSE
Scary stories often reflect terrors from the history of the cultures or countries that gave birth to them. This is a prime example. The Civil War was a time of unspeakable death and tragedy in American history. It's not a surprise it inspired so many scary stories from American folklore.

Source: Musick, Ruth Ann. *The Telltale Lilac Bush and Other West Virginia Ghost Tales*, The University Press of Kentucky, 1965

A BABY IN THE WOODS
Many people have thought of the wilderness as the home of devilish creatures since the Book of Genesis (and probably earlier). This is just one more creepy tale from folklore in which a seemingly innocent being in the woods turns out to be something much more sinister. Read Nathaniel Hawthorne's "Young Goodman Brown" or Stephen King's excellent "The Man in the Black Suit" for more detailed stories of this nature.

Source: San Souci, Robert D. *More Short & Shivery*, Yearling, 1994

THE HANDPRINT
From Shakespeare's "Macbeth" to Poe's "The Tell-Tale Heart" (and plenty others), we have many stories in which the blood someone has shed will continue to haunt the living until justice is served. It's a trope that appears throughout world literature and folklore.

Alvin Schwartz often used Helen Creighton's *Bluenose Ghosts* as a source for his *Scary Stories to Tell in the Dark Books*. I've done the same here. Anyone who enjoys these books should make a point of reading it.

Source: Creighton, Helen. *Bluenose Ghosts*, Helen Creighton, 1976

THE SAILOR'S VISIT
"The Sailor's Visit" is another version of a story in which a loved one visits at the time of their death. This story was worth including because the detail of the sailor's footprints adds a uniquely haunting quality. Like "A Ship in the Ice," this story also reflects the dangers of sea voyages, and the anxieties of those whose loved ones took such voyages to earn a living.

Source: Creighton, Helen. *Bluenose Ghosts*, Helen Creighton, 1976

THE TUNNELS
The Odessa Catacombs are a series of tunnels beneath the city of Odessa in Ukraine. As this retelling touches on, they came to be when a period of frequent construction in Odessa resulted in a need for construction materials. Various people and companies created individual mines to provide these materials. Over time, the tunnels of the mines began to connect. They now make up one of the largest underground mazes in the world.

The story of Masha's disappearance in the tunnels is actually fairly recent. Although it doesn't seem to be true, it spread across the Internet, and now many believe it is true regardless.

It might even be true in a way. Masha might not have been a real person, but there are a few accounts of people exploring the tunnels, getting lost, and dying of hunger and starvation.

This is one more story that serves as an important reminder: folklore doesn't end. Decades from now, people might still tell the tale of Masha's death. I wanted to include it in this collection because it reveals how the tradition of telling scary stories hasn't ended. In fact, thanks to the Internet, that tradition may be more prevalent than ever.

Source: Pearl, Mike. "The Enduring Legend of the Girl Who Died in Odessa's Catacombs." *Vice*, Vice Media Group, 27 October 2015

ABOUT THE AUTHOR & ILLUSTRATOR

Joe Oliveto is a freelance writer currently living in Brooklyn, NY. His lifelong obsession with scary stories inspired him to write this series, which he plans to continue. He's also teaching himself how to draw, and hopes the next editions feature even creepier illustrations. You can contact him at Joseph.Oliveto@gmail.com.